Unchained Courage

A Whitcomb Springs Story

MK McClintock

The Whitcomb Springs series title and concept were created by MK McClintock.

Copyright © 2018 MK McClintock
All rights reserved.
Trappers Peak Publishing
Bigfork, Montana

Published and printed in the United States of America

McClintock, MK
"Forsaken Trail"; short story/MK McClintock

Cover design by MK McClintock
Cover Image Background by Ryan Tanguilan | Shutterstock
Cover Image Eagle by MK McClintock

For Uncle Jim,
and all those who have served
with honor and courage.

Unchained Courage

Whitcomb Springs, Montana Territory
July 4, 1865

DANIEL LED HIS HORSE over the familiar two-mile ride up the mountain trail. He reached a small clearing, and in the center a lake spread out in glistening glory, reflecting the mountain peaks behind it. He dismounted and stared in awe at the vista as his speckled horse grazed. Images of Evelyn overlapped his vision until it seemed a transparent silhouette of her smiling face hovered over the mountains.

A well-kept cabin stood a dozen yards from the crystal-clear lake. The stream feeding into it from the north flowed out to the east and created a short waterfall down a slope of rocks. Cooper McCord, the man who had been by Evelyn's side while Daniel had been at war, called this part of paradise home when he wasn't in town.

Cooper's friendship had become a steadying hand

in the three months since Daniel's return. Without speaking of it, Cooper understood what Daniel had been through. They never spoke of their experiences: Daniel's in the war between the North and South, and Cooper's from his days serving as a civilian tracker in the army, occupying the West and witnessing the travesties wrought against the natives.

Cooper first brought Daniel to this same mountain lake a week after the nightmares had begun. Since then, Daniel had found solace in this place high above the town, the people, the noise. When he craved silence, he came here. Daniel had seen the disappointment in Evelyn's eyes when he remained quiet about his experiences, but she never pushed.

He heard the crunch of horse hooves on rocks and twigs covering the trail. Only Cooper came here—it was his home. Daniel wondered where he had been for the past three days.

Daniel did turn when Cooper said nothing and saw the extra horse with the large buck draped over the saddle and covered in heavy canvas. Cooper walked over and stood next to Daniel. The dawn's warm sun promised a clear and sunny day.

"Thought you might be here this morning."

"The buck is for tonight?"

Cooper nodded. "Evelyn will understand if you

aren't there."

"I can't do that to her." Daniel watched the sun inch higher on the horizon. The first Independence Day in four years without the screams, trumpets, cannons, and muskets echoing in his ears. Instead of a body-strewn battlefield, Daniel gazed upon the most beautiful valley he'd ever seen in his life. Instead of cries coming from a hospital tent, the town of Whitcomb Springs below was a haven for him and anyone else seeking solace and a peaceful place to live.

Daniel still heard the screams in his nightmares. Muskets firing, filling the air with the stench of smoke and death. He relived it often. Most nights, the comfort of holding his wife was enough to waylay the madness within, but the worst of the memories sneaked through his barrier.

"She doesn't ask about it."

Cooper said nothing for a few seconds, and then, "She may not. Your wife never asked me about my days in the army, not once in four years."

"What about Abigail? Have you spoken with her about those years?" Daniel watched Cooper toss a pebble down the mountain.

Cooper nodded. "I couldn't court her without telling her everything. It wasn't easy. You've been back three months, and what you went through is nothing even I can imagine. Give it time."

"And did it help, telling Abigail?"

"Nothing has brought me more peace before or since."

Daniel kept his eyes focused on the rising sun. Soon it would be high enough to bring light to the entire valley. Where they sat, the mountain shielded them in its shadow. Turning to Cooper, he asked, "Do you ever regret not going?"

"Sometimes."

"I'm grateful you stayed, for what you did for Evelyn and this town." Daniel stood and walked back to his horse. It had remained close yet still wandered to find the sweetest grass with morning dew. "If I had known how long I would have been away—"

"No one knew how long it would last." Cooper also walked back to his horse, checking to make sure the large buck was still secure on the second animal. "And if our roles had been reversed, you would have done the same."

Daniel studied his friend. "Evelyn tells me you've been spending a lot of time with her sister."

Cooper grinned at him, and though Daniel reciprocated the smile, his heart remained heavy with too many memories. He lived in a constant fog with only glimpses of light, a brightness he found with

Evelyn, but still the darkness remained beneath the surface, waiting to rise at unexpected times.

"Abigail is special. I love her, and I only tell you this so you know my intentions are honorable."

Daniel pulled himself into the saddle. "If I doubted that, I would have done something about you a long time ago." This time his sincere smile blew away some of the darker clouds as he headed down the mountain trail toward home.

THE TOWN WAS QUIET as expected this time of morning, and yet an eerie silence filled the air like the mist still dispersed over the valley floor. He and Cooper traveled down from the mountain on a trail that connected to the north road leading into town. A hard-packed dirt road passed by Daniel and Evelyn's home, where Evelyn and Abigail could often be found in the garden at this early hour.

Evelyn doted on her flower gardens, but this morning the flowers stood alone, glistening with water droplets in the early morning light. The town's shared vegetable garden to the south of the house was also empty, tools set against the fence with no one to yield them.

"Mr. Whitcomb!" Cody Skeeters jumped up and

down on the front porch of the big house and ran toward them. "Mrs. Whitcomb says I ain't supposed to move until you and Cooper get here!"

Daniel held up a hand and looked down at the boy. "Is she hurt?"

Cody shook his head. "There's a dead man, Mr. Whitcomb! A real dead man. I ain't never seen nothing like it."

"Come here, Cody." Cooper motioned the boy closer. "Where is he?"

Cody pointed toward town. "In the clearing next to Miss Maggie's saloon."

"You take this pack horse down to Mr. Andris at the blacksmith's barn. Can you do that for me?"

The boy nodded, his eyes still wide from excitement, and clasped the reins Cooper passed to him.

"Is Miss Abigail with her sister?"

Cody shook his head again. "I ain't seen Miss Abigail."

Both men urged their horses forward. Most of the townspeople had yet to leave their homes, which Daniel considered a blessing. His horse skidded to a halt a short distance from where a few early risers had gathered near the grass next to the saloon that also doubled as a restaurant, if one didn't need variety. The saloon didn't serve much beyond stew and biscuits or meatloaf, but it was one of the best meals in town.

He spotted Maggie Lynch, the proprietor, on the front boardwalk of the Blackwater Tavern, named after the pub her grandfather once operated in Ireland. Her wild, flame-red hair curled around her head and shoulders.

Daniel searched the faces but did not see his wife. His heart rate accelerated, as it always did when he thought of Evelyn in possible danger, and he pushed his way through the small circle of people.

He saw Evelyn kneeling on the ground next to a prone body covered with a canvas tarp. Daniel touched her shoulder, and when she looked at him, it was with damp and worried eyes. He helped his wife stand and took her place next to the body. Daniel inched the canvas away from the head, careful to block what he uncovered. Whitcomb Springs still awaited the new doctor, but the dead man did not need healing.

"What happened?"

No one immediately answered his question. Daniel heard Cooper move up beside him and ask, "Where's Abigail?"

"She's all right, Cooper. She went to the school early to prepare and doesn't know this has happened." Evelyn added, "Maggie found the body about a half hour ago. We wanted to move him, but then thought you and Daniel should see him first."

Daniel didn't yet know everyone in town, and from his appearance, he suspected the young man worked in the mine or timber camp. Cooper confirmed his suspicions.

"That's Jacob Smith. He was hired the start of this season at the mine." Cooper squatted and ran a hand along the back of Jacob's head to what appeared to be the source of the blood. "Feels like someone hit him. Had to have been a powerful blow to kill him."

Daniel looked up at his wife who now stood next to Maggie. He asked Maggie, "Did you or anyone else see what happened?"

Maggie shook her head. "I saw nothing. We don't open for hours so no one else was inside. I came outside to go walking, like I always do first thing, and saw Jacob instead."

"You know him?"

"Sure do," Maggie said. "He came into the saloon once a week for the meatloaf. Sweet kid, only nineteen years old."

"He dreamed of becoming a rancher," Evelyn said, another reminder at how much more Evelyn was connected to the town than he. Daniel helped wherever he could, went to church, frequented the businesses, but he realized he'd yet to allow himself to become a part of the town the way his wife had. He wasn't yet ready. A young man he never met—one of his employees—lay dead on the streets of his town. Daniel's days of mourning the years he'd lost to war were about to be over. Time to focus on the now.

The sun's path into the morning sky continued. Many who lived in town or nearby would soon appear. Men on the first shift at the timber camp would already be at work, and the mine would open for the day. Daniel shared a glance with Cooper, who nodded once and rose. Cooper pointed to two of them men standing nearby. "Help me carry him to the clinic."

One man felt it necessary to speak the obvious. "But there ain't no doc there."

"No, there isn't." Cooper motioned them over when Daniel moved out of the way. "But it's empty, close, and we have to get him off the street."

Daniel waited for them to carry the young man across the road before he faced his wife and Maggie. "You have an extra room over your saloon, is that right, Maggie?" He caught the look shared between the two women.

"I do."

"I'd feel better if your brother stayed with you until we find out what happened. I'm sure he wouldn't mind leaving the timber camp for a few days."

Maggie's eyes narrowed and Daniel looked to Evelyn for help. "Maggie, Daniel's right, it will only be for a short time, and it would ease my worry."

"Of all the—"

Cooper's return interrupted the start of Maggie's tirade.

"He has a point, Maggie. This happened in front of your saloon. Might not be a coincidence."

"If I agree to this, I'm doing it for Evelyn." She pointed a finger at Cooper's chest.

"Understood, Maggie."

"We've got him! We've got the killer!" The shouts came from outside the circle of people, now parting to allow the newcomers passage to the center.

Daniel and Cooper watched a tall, black man being dragged toward them by two miners Daniel had met soon after his return home. Daniel stared in shock. Before him, hands bound and blood on his shirt stood Gordon Wells, the former slave who had saved his life.

DANIEL REACHED FOR GORDON'S bound hands and pulled him away from the men who had brought him forward. "This man is not a killer." Daniel untied Gordon's hands and said to the crowd, "Unless you have definitive proof that this man has done anything wrong, he'll be released until we can investigate.

One of the would-be captors said while pointing at Gordon, "We have no sheriff, and I know what's right in front of me. He's got blood on his shirt."

Daniel knew most of the residents were still getting used to him. Evelyn had been the matriarch of Whitcomb Springs for four years, and many of the people now living and working for them had only ever heard of the man who went off to fight in the war. Daniel remembered the accuser's name—Abraham— but nothing else about him.

Cooper eased the man back a few paces from Daniel and Gordon. "Do you trust me, Abraham?"

Abraham pulled his gaze away and glanced at Cooper. "I do. You saved me when my leg got caught under a beam in the mine."

"Then trust me to investigate what happened here. If Daniel knows and trusts this man, that should be good enough for all of us."

Abraham faced Daniel again, this time with wariness visible in his eyes, before he walked away.

"Daniel?"

He held out a hand for his wife. "Evelyn, I'd like you to meet Gordon Wells."

Daniel watched moisture gather in Evelyn's eyes.

Without hesitation, she embraced the man's hands. "Thank you for saving my husband's life."

"I feared somethin' bad when dey found me. I sure am glad you is here, Mr. Whitcomb."

Cooper handled the few people who had remained to watch the drama unfold and told them to go about their own business. They had a town supper to get ready for that evening. Daniel and Evelyn had celebrated their country's day of independence every year when they'd been at home. When they ventured west, they'd had only one year of peace before Daniel left, and the celebrating ceased. Most of the people dispersed, casting curious glances toward the Whitcombs and the newcomer, but neither Daniel or Evelyn paid them any mind.

"You used to call me Daniel. I hope you'll do so again." He looked to Maggie and asked, "May we use your saloon for a few minutes?"

"Of course. You go right on in and I'll make sure no one disturbs you. Lord sake's, I never imagined something like this happening here." Maggie shook her head and ushered them inside, closing the double doors behind them.

Evelyn rushed behind the long, polished bar and returned with a glass of water for Gordon. "Please, sit and rest."

Eyes wide and hesitant, Gordon circled his large hand around the glass and gulped down half the contents. "I thank you, ma'am."

Daniel remained standing next Gordon, waited a few minutes for his old friend to regain his bearings.

"I done caused you folks trouble."

"No, you haven't." Daniel pulled a chair out for his wife before he moved one so he could sit and face Gordon. "Tell me what's happened. The blood on your shirt is drying, but still fresh. You've got a cut on your lip, but I know it didn't come from killing anyone. No one who goes to the trouble of saving a person would take a life without good reason."

"I was huntin' for my family. We is camped maybe two miles from here."

"You were coming to Whitcomb Springs?"

Gordon glanced briefly at Evelyn. "Yes, ma'am. I remember Mr.—Daniel here sayin' how if I wanted, I ought to come. There weren't nothin' else for our family where we was, so here we is."

"I meant it, and I hoped you would find your way here." Daniel glanced toward the door as new shouting ensued. "We need to see that your family is brought safely to town. Your wife and daughter, correct?"

Gordon nodded. "Dey is waiting for me. I walked more'n I thought following the deer."

"Where did they find you?"

"I realized how close I came to town and thought to borrow a horse from de blacksmith. Dat's when dem two men found me. The blood is from the deer I left in de woods."

"I believe you, Gordon." Daniel's eyes met his wife's, and an unspoken understanding passed between them. "Your family won't understand if someone shows up in your stead. We'll leave out the back and go to them together. My horse is out front, but we need our wagon."

Evelyn said, "I'll take your horse back to the house."

Daniel looked over his shoulder and through the windows at the front of the saloon. A larger crowd now gathered, curious about the red-stained grass. None of them looked inside but rather to where the body had lain. That would soon change. Daniel knew most folks in town cared more about truth and kindness than speculation, but a few wouldn't be generous to Gordon's presence after losing some of their own in a fight believed by some to solely be about ending slavery. It wasn't Gordon's fault, yet fear and bigotry too often clouded initial reactions. For some, their judgment began and ended with ignorance.

"Leave the horse. I'll saddle another when we get to the barn."

Evelyn nodded and pointed toward the back door. "I'll wait a few seconds before going out front with Maggie."

"Tell Cooper where we've gone, just in case we are not back in two hours. It shouldn't take longer than that to get there and return." Daniel squeezed his wife's hand and led Gordon out the rear door. He glanced back once at Evelyn before making sure the area was clear. The short line of businesses on the one main road in town backed up to the Whitcomb's land, only part of it treed. They didn't have to worry about coming across anyone else, but someone might still see them crossing behind the community garden to the barn.

Daniel prayed everyone remained distracted enough as they ran, hunched over, toward the barn.

EVELYN STEPPED ONTO THE front porch of the saloon as quietly as possible, closing the door behind her. She nodded once to Cooper, who stood nearby answering questions as they were asked from the few who remained behind. Most people had left as told, but Evelyn wanted no one else around when she informed Cooper where Daniel and Gordon had gone.

A few folks came and went. Others who had recently awakened or ventured into town stopped out of curiosity. News of a dead man, especially one many of them knew, spread quicker than a wildfire on the prairie. No one paid much attention to Evelyn or Maggie, but Evelyn knew it wouldn't be long before someone noticed and wondered what the women were doing.

Evelyn leaned closer to Maggie. "I need to find Abigail, tell her what's happened. This won't be contained long, and soon there will be speculation about Gordon's whereabouts. We need to give him and Daniel time to return with Gordon's family."

Maggie perused the crowd and waved to a pair of women Evelyn recognized as new in town with their miner husbands. Maggie said, "You find your sister. How long does Daniel need?"

"He said two hours."

Maggie nodded. "I'll handle things here with Cooper, deflect inquiries for as long as possible."

Evelyn laid a hand on Maggie's arm in a gentle gesture of appreciation. "Thank you, Maggie. This man accused of murder, he saved Daniel's life. I cannot allow anyone—"

Maggie covered Evelyn's hand and squeezed. "I understand. If that boy was killed, and we don't know for certain he was, I'd rather believe no one would do such a thing. Go now, but slowly so as not to draw attention."

By way of distraction, Maggie walked the length of the saloon porch until she perched on the top step that led down to the grassy area where the body had been discovered. She drew any curious onlookers' gazes to her, giving Evelyn time to make her way to the school.

Evelyn did not cross paths with anyone on her way to the meadow where the school was situated near a brook. The serenity of the setting belied the morning's events. What began as a peaceful day, a day of celebration for their country, turned into a tragedy. Evelyn had prayed for calm and peace for Daniel's sake.

He'd blessedly spent the previous evening free of nightmares, but she longed for a time when weeks or months would pass without the terrors of war revisiting him in slumber. He did not speak of their years apart in detail and she did not ask. She soothed him while he slept, allowing him to return to sleep without knowing his own anguish. Other nights, they awoke together, Daniel dripping with sweat and Evelyn trying to ease her racing heart. On those nights, Daniel left their bed to stand outside in the cool, night air, returning only when his breathing had calmed.

Evelyn picked up her pace as she approached the schoolhouse, shaking the thoughts of hopelessness away. Abigail sat at the scarred-top desk at the front of the small room when Evelyn pushed in through the double door.

They knew each other so well, Evelyn and her sister. Abigail immediately stood and hurried to meet Evelyn halfway.

"What's happened?"

Evelyn tried to ease the worry lines from her face, but from the expression her sister wore, she'd been unsuccessful. "Jacob Smith, a young miner, died sometime this morning in the clearing next to Maggie's saloon."

Abigail squeezed her sister's hands. "I knew Jacob. He came to me only yesterday to ask if I could teach him how to read." Abigail's chest heaved with heavy breaths.

Evelyn eased her into one of the student's seats. "There's more, I'm afraid. Do you remember Daniel mentioned a man named Gordon Wells?"

Abigail nodded. "The slave who saved him near the end of the war."

"That's right. Daniel told Gordon to come to Whitcomb Springs should he ever wish to start anew. Well, Gordon has arrived, and one of the miners dragged him into town this morning."

"And he's suspected in the murder."

Evelyn raised a brow at her sister. "How did you

guess?"

"I heard stories during the war about the mistreatment of slaves. How even those who did nothing wrong were considered criminals. People do not change so quickly, nor do they forget." Abigail stood now on steadier legs. "Gordon has unfortunate timing."

"Yes, although I believe he decided to come here when Daniel first offered."

"Then he's been traveling for some time. Does he have family with him?" Abigail asked.

"He does, a wife and daughter. They'll be staying with us for now."

Evelyn watched her sister's expression of understanding turn to one of disbelief.

Abigail said, "By the way you're looking at me, you seem to believe that will bother me. You forget, Evie, I was closer to the conflicts. Still protected, yes, but I witnessed men and women being smuggled into the North. No one should have to live with so much fear."

Evelyn blinked a few times. "You said nothing. To be close enough to see, you would have been helping . . . Oh, dear. I assume no one knew."

"Yes, I assisted at a stop on the Underground Railroad. I brought food and other supplies to help those newly arrived. For our family's sake, I kept some distance, but I would not be stopped from helping."

Evelyn blinked again, this time to keep tears of both belated worry and pride from escaping. She cleared her throat and composed herself before saying, "Part of why I came to tell you is so you're not surprised if parents keep their children from class today when they hear of what's happened. Some of them will hesitate to let the young ones wander far from their sides. We will need your help to calm the ripple effects of conjecture."

"Should I close the school for a few days?"

Evelyn glanced at the silver watch fob attached to her apron, the apron she still wore when she was interrupted in the garden earlier. She considered both the benefits and the consequences of keeping the children away and shook her head. "Parents who live outside town will not hear of Jacob's death before school begins. Many of their children walk to town alone and it is better that they have a place to go."

"Of course. Please let me know when Daniel returns."

"I will."

"And Evie?"

Evelyn turned back to face her sister.

"Was anyone else injured?"

Evelyn understood the unspoken question. "Cooper returned with Daniel this morning. He is safe."

DANIEL AND GORDON REACHED the Wells's camp by way of the main road. Travelers rarely journeyed to and from Whitcomb Springs since the stage did not yet stop in their valley, but as word of the timber and mining jobs spread throughout the territory, men and families came in search of work.

Someday the stage, and perhaps a spur line, would benefit their small town, but today, Daniel was grateful they lived at the end of a less traveled road. Daniel noticed the smoke from a campfire before Gordon indicated they'd arrived. The camp was not visible from the road, but Gordon whistled twice and half a minute later a woman and child emerged from the trees.

They smiled when Gordon climbed down from the buckboard's seat, but gave pause when they noticed Daniel atop his horse. He remained in the saddle until after Gordon embraced them and explained Daniel's presence. Gordon's wife, Hany Wells, took a few tentative steps toward Daniel's horse. After almost of minute of studying him, she waved him down to join them.

Daniel witnessed what the slaves had suffered at the hands of their masters, yet he still could not imagine the depths of their fear when confronted by a white man. He did not fool himself into believing their journey to Montana had been without great difficulty and unease.

Hany was a handsome woman with round, brown eyes, wide smile, and a complexion one shade lighter than her husband's. She wore her dark, loosely curled hair at her nape, and took pains to straighten her frayed apron. Their daughter was as becoming as her mother.

Daniel approached the family out of respect and surprised them all. "It is indeed a pleasure to meet you, Mrs. Wells."

When Hany smiled, Daniel believed it was with sincerity. "It's nice to meet you, Mr. Whitcomb. This here is our girl, Grace. Gordon's done talked about you all de way here. But how is you here, Mr. Whitcomb?"

"Please, call me Daniel." He looked to Gordon before responding to the question. "There's been trouble in town. Nothing to alarm you," he assured her, "but it is best if we return. Is your camp easy to pack up?"

Hany nodded, but Daniel did not miss the concerned glance she cast toward her husband. "Is you in trouble, Gordon?"

"I reckon maybe so, Hany, but Mr.—Daniel—say I's not to worry. We is close now, Hany. We is real close."

Hany's doubt showed on her face when she looked at Daniel. "Is that de truth?"

"I promise, you will all be safe. I will explain on the way, but let us hurry now."

EVELYN TENDED TO HER flowers, though her heart was not in the work. She pulled a weed and then an herb, not noticing the difference until the healthy plant hung from her fingers, dirt crumbling back to earth. Evelyn replanted the herb, taking care to cover the roots again.

She looked up every time she heard someone on the road, each time reminding herself they would not come through town, yet she continued to look and hope. Two hours had come and gone, and still the day had not yet shifted from morning.

Cooper and two men he'd chosen were watching over the body. Poor Jacob Smith would need to be prepared for burial. The nights brought cooler air but the days burned warm, and they could not leave him aboveground for more than a day or two.

After her visit with Abigail, she'd spent an hour assuring families who inquired that there was no danger to anyone, only she wished the words held more conviction. They did not know who killed one of their own or why. She hoped everyone would follow Maggie's lead and believe no one among them could kill another. Jacob was a young man and hard worker. He would not have had much on him except his weekly earnings, distributed the day before to all of the miners. The men working timber and building the new sawmill would receive their pay today, which led Evelyn to doubt one of their workers had done this.

"Evelyn?"

She glanced up and saw the mine foreman's wife approach the fence. "Mrs. Cosgrove."

"Is it true what I've just heard, Evelyn?"

"Yes, Lillian, I'm afraid it is."

"In our town, a murderer is running loose. It's not to be borne, Evelyn."

Lillian Cosgrove preferred city life to the small mountain valley, but this was where her husband had come so it's where she lived.

"Oh, Lillian, there is not a killer loose among us, and I do not believe anyone else is in danger. Cooper and Daniel will discover what happened, and in the meantime, is our energy not better spent on prayers for the departed?"

"Well, of course, but—"

"And should we not be mindful of the town's children, assuring them that there is nothing to fear?

Your own daughter will want to know you are not concerned, is that not true?"

"Yes, it is, but we need a proper sheriff."

Evelyn used the trowel to help stand from the flower bed. She gave her apron a cursory dusting. "We have a proper sheriff. Mr. Jenkins has accepted the position and will arrive any day now."

"But it has been more than a month since he accepted. Surely someone else is interested in the position."

"We received other replies, but none as qualified as Abbott Jenkins. He's leaving the Pinkertons to come here. We want to be sure we have the best for our town, for the people. Do you not agree?"

Lillian's bodice swelled when she stood straighter and inhaled deeply. Her chin rose a fraction higher than necessary. "I do agree."

"The committee to hire a new schoolteacher could do with another member."

The other woman's demeanor shifted in quick degrees. Evelyn knew many of the townspeople's idiosyncrasies and weaknesses, and Lillian's weakness was her desire for recognition and control. She meant well, and Evelyn had learned to handle Lillian, and the few others like her, with care.

"Are you asking me?"

Lillian knew what Evelyn meant, but Evelyn still acknowledged her with a nod. "We would be pleased to have you on the committee."

"Then it would be my honor."

Evelyn hid a smile. "It won't be easy finding someone to fill the post, so you must be patient."

"I will be ready." Lillian pressed a hand to her corset-held middle and fluttered away in better spirits than when she'd arrived. Evelyn believed the good mood would last only a few minutes, until Lillian remembered why she had visited Evelyn in the first place.

Evelyn heard what she'd been waiting for and was slow to move, waving to Lillian when she glanced over her shoulder. When no one else was around, Evelyn picked up her tools and carried them to the shed near the edge of the garden. In her peripheral, she observed movement and recognized Daniel's tall frame. The others were a blur when they hurried into the barn.

The buckboard remained outside, and a minute later Daniel reemerged to take care of the wagon and horses. Evelyn said his name when she was still a dozen feet away, so as not to startle him, but he must have already sensed her presence for he turned toward her.

"They are safe?"

He nodded and brought her into his arms. "They

are. Frightened, but doing well considering."

"Did Gordon tell her what happened?"

"Some of it, but not all because of their daughter. Her name is Grace. She's a sweet girl."

Evelyn heard the wistfulness in her husband's voice. "We'll have one of our own someday. We can fill the house with laughter and love."

Daniel smoothed a hand over his gelding's flank and removed the saddle. "Someday."

Evelyn reminded herself that he wanted children as much as she did, but fear continued to grip him, fear of his own mortality, and fear that the scars he carried home with him would pass onto their son or daughter. They had tried and failed in the past. She held her counsel and leaned up to press a kiss to his cheek. "I'll prepare food for them. It's safe to bring them into the house now. "

"Is Harriet here?"

Evelyn shook her head in question to the young widow who often worked at the Whitcomb's house to help with the housekeeping and gardens. "She's helping Abigail at the school today, and I'll let her and Tabitha know they won't be needed around here the remainder of the week. I preferred not to have anyone around before you came back, and I don't want our guests to be uncomfortable. I informed Abigail that

Gordon and his family would stay here for a few days." Evelyn noticed now only one additional horse, a tired creature who deserved a permanent home in a grassy pasture. "Did they travel all this way with only the one animal?"

"They did. Gordon walked most of the way."

"And so far." Evelyn brushed a tear as soon as it fell on her cheek. "I won't be long. We need not wait until darkness comes to bring them inside. I've been watching, and there is no one about. Those who are in town are more curious about what happened to Jacob."

"Then word hasn't gotten out about Gordon?"

"I have not heard talk of it. The miner who first accused Gordon should be working. Cooper is at the clinic; I told him where you'd gone."

Evelyn kept a brisk pace on her walk back to the house and felt Daniel's eyes on her the entire way. She stopped and walked past her husband to the barn. When she entered, the three inhabitants moved deeper into a corner until Gordon recognized Evelyn.

"Hello, Mrs. Whitcomb."

"Please, Gordon, it's Evelyn."

"Yes, ma'am. This here is my missus, Hany, and our girl, Grace."

Evelyn held her hand out to Gordon's wife, and only after gentle prodding from her husband did Hany accept the gesture of friendship. "It is my honor to meet you, Mrs. Wells, and your beautiful daughter. Your husband saved my life, too, when he saved Mr. Whitcomb."

"De good Lord was watchin' over them both dat day."

"Yes, He was. Now, I've prepared rooms in the house for you. If Grace prefers not to have her own room right now, then Daniel can bring a cot into your bedroom. We'll get you settled into a place of your own soon. For a few days, I hope you will consent to be our guests."

Both Gordon and Hany looked flabbergasted. Gordon said, "We is fine in de barn."

"I won't hear of it."

"She never loses an argument, Gordon," Daniel said from behind Evelyn.

Gordon merely nodded and whispered something for only his wife to hear. Their daughter Grace, who appeared six or seven, tugged on her mother's arm, and said in a barely perceptible voice, "Are we home now, Mama?"

Hany raised cautious and hopeful eyes to Evelyn and Daniel. "I suspect we is, Gracie girl."

"WE'LL NEED TO CANCEL the celebration tonight."

Daniel watched his wife prepare tea. Her quick hands and long fingers didn't waste a movement. They were alone in the kitchen while the Wells family rested upstairs in the guest rooms. Young Grace had preferred to stay with her parents, until she saw the big bed that was offered to her. She had approached the bed with shy wonder, running her hand over the colorful quilt Evelyn had made her second winter in Montana. It proved to be a pleasant and useful hobby that helped pass the time during the long, cold months. Daniel recalled his surprise upon seeing that quilt, and three others, when he arrived, and even more surprise when Evelyn confessed she'd made them. Her skills had always been more academic and in managing a household, rather than in domestic pursuits.

Cooper had sent a note by way of young Cody Skeeters that they would prepare the ground for Jacob's burial.

Daniel returned his thoughts to her comment and offered one of his own. "I'm not certain we should cancel."

Evelyn set the teapot on the linen-covered table and stared at him. "Jacob Smith will need to be buried tomorrow. How can we celebrate anything with what's happened?"

Jacob's was not the first suspect death Daniel had ever witnessed. Desperate men committed abominable crimes, and in the past four years, Daniel had seen too many desperate men. When the only stories he carried with him were of death and destruction, it was impossible to share those missing years with Evelyn.

"We make it a celebration of Jacob's life, of his dreams. We celebrate in his honor and in the town's future."

"It is a wonderful idea, but I feel that is not your only purpose."

"No, it's not." Daniel accepted the cup of fragrant tea. "I need to be certain no one else comes looking for Gordon. He did not do this, and I promised his family he would be safe. I expect just about everyone who lives and works in Whitcomb Springs to attend. Whoever isn't . . . Well, that will be telling."

"You're going to meet Cooper."

Evelyn always seemed to know Daniel's thoughts and plans before he did. "I am. I won't be long, but I need to see this through. It is time for me to look after this town, the way you and Cooper have."

"You do, Daniel."

"Not in the way I should. I labor and we give money where needed to help the town grow, but I have not allowed myself to become a part of this place, these people, not like when we first arrived." Daniel drank a bit of the tea to placate Evelyn. When he pushed back his chair and stood, he eased her into his embrace. "I promise you, I will no longer be a ghost."

Without waiting for a reply, he pressed his lips to hers, allowing himself to savor and memorize everything her nearness made him feel, and he left.

DANIEL ENTERED THE CLINIC and closed the door behind him. Cooper nodded once to Daniel before returning his attention to Jacob. A fresh canvas had been placed over the body, and only his head and arm were uncovered.

The building boasted a generous front room, a back office, and like most businesses in town, comfortable living quarters on the second floor. They had equipped the clinic with all the basic accoutrements of a doctor's office, and planned to leave the remaining details to the physician, when they found one.

"How is Gordon and his family?"

"They're resting and understandably worried. When I was still in nursery school, my father spoke of slavery in the South and explained that no man had the right to own another. I remember agreeing with him, but I never—never—understood what any of it meant until I met Gordon. Even those first few years of war, I was still in the North. When Gordon saved me, knowing the consequences, he taught me more about freedom and fairness than I'd learned at any point in my life." Daniel had been staring at the body laid out on the long table in the center of the office. He had not meant to say so much and was grateful when Cooper kept silent. "Have you found anything?"

Cooper motioned Daniel over. "It sure would be easier if a doctor was here to look him over, but there's no mistaking this." Cooper raised Jacob's arm and pushed up the sleeve. Daniel studied the unmistakable double punctures of a snake bite. The arm had swelled around the bite.

"Rattlesnake."

"That's what it looks like. We rarely spot a prairie rattler up here, and we've never had someone in town bit by one. I've seen this before, though." Colton lowered Jacob's arm. "I checked the bump on the back of his head again. It could have happened from a hard fall off his horse. If he was bit, he might not have been able to stay in the saddle."

"You think it's possible he was bit, got on his horse to come into town, and fell."

"Better explanation than someone we know maybe killed him. We'd have to find his horse to confirm the theory."

Daniel felt the back of Jacob's head. "Have you looked around again where he was found?"

"Yes, but I'm not sure it helps too much. There are few rocks there, one with blood that could have killed him when he landed. I relieved two men from the mine today to stand by and make sure no one disturbed the area. Folks have mostly moved on now. A lot of them are still asking questions. I've let it get around that this was an accident. Hope I'm right."

"So do I." Daniel raised the canvas over Jacob's face. "Whether or not he fell, he would have died from the bite. There's no one around here with medical knowledge enough to have saved him from the venom."

"I've treated a few snake bites, though his arm looks like he was too far gone already." Cooper walked around the body toward the door. "We need to find Jacob's horse. It should have stayed close."

Daniel stepped outside with Cooper. Someone had positioned two more men at either end of the wide porch in front of the clinic. Daniel acknowledged both and said to Cooper, "That no one has seen or found the horse yet is worrying. Stolen, perhaps?"

"I'm thinking so. Jacob bought his horse from Dominik Andris last week."

"Do you remember what the horse looks like?"

Cooper nodded. "If he's wandering loose, we'll find him."

"It's more likely the horse was taken." Daniel rubbed a hand over the back of his neck and looked toward the mountains. "I don't believe there's a killer amongst us, but theft is another matter. We've hired on a few new people the past month, still strangers. If we don't locate the animal, our next step will be to see who of the men have left unexpectedly."

When Cooper didn't answer, Daniel glanced his way and followed the direction of his attention—the school. "Have you spoken with Abigail yet today?"

"It was the first thing I had planned to do this morning, and then this happened."

"Go and see her. Harriett is helping at the school, so Abigail can step away for a few minutes."

Cooper murmured an affirmation of Daniel's suggestion, yet made no move to leave. Daniel considered his friend and confidant carefully, recognizing Cooper's indecision for what it truly was. Daniel said, "You had other plans for tonight, important plans, didn't you?"

"I did."

"I spoke with Evelyn earlier, and it seems to me that tonight's celebration should move forward. If we can assure everyone that Jacob's death was an accident, we can celebrate the day in honor of him, of all the men who have been lost. Jacob was young and eager and a soldier deserving of a nobler way to leave this life. I don't want another year passing without us having reason to celebrate our independence. It's important."

He anticipated Cooper's surprise. Daniel explained, "Evelyn told me that Jacob fought for the Confederacy."

"Does it bother you, knowing he was on the other side?"

"It might have, in the beginning. It wasn't long into the war when I realized that most men on both sides didn't want to be there. We kept going, fighting, killing . . ." Daniel shook the memory of the last battle from his thoughts. "No, it doesn't matter." He slapped Cooper on the shoulder, a friendly and masculine gesture meant to show affection. It was the only closeness Daniel could get to people these days—everyone except Evelyn. "I'll see if anyone didn't show up for their shift at the mine or timber camp." This time he offered his friend a smile. "Make sure you go and see Abigail before you look for Jacob's horse. And Cooper, you should ask her to step outside. You still smell like three days on the trail."

As EVELYN STEPPED AWAY from the clinic, she saw Cooper walking toward the schoolhouse. He had a lead on her but she was saved from an undignified shout when a woman stopped him. When Evelyn closed the distance between them, she called his name.

Cooper and the woman—Nettie Sandstrom, a newcomer to town with her husband—turned toward her. "Evelyn."

Evelyn smiled at Nettie and offered her hand. Though her errand was one of urgency, her position to help maintain calm was paramount. "How are you and your husband settling in, Nettie?"

"Oh, we're settling in just fine, Mrs. Whitcomb. The welcome basket you brought over was the nicest thing, and everyone here has been so kind. I was convinced Taylor had plumb lost his mind when he told me about this place. I was happy in Salt Lake City, but I'm glad he convinced me to come."

Evelyn retrieved her hand from Nettie's enthusiastic grip and kept her smile trained on the young woman. Nineteen-year-old Nettie and twenty-year-old Taylor Sandstrom reminded Evelyn of her and Daniel when they first dreamed of what their future might hold. "Whitcomb Springs is lucky to have you."

Nettie's smile wavered, her glance darting from Evelyn to Cooper and back again. "Mr. McCord says there's no cause to worry over what happened with that poor miner this morning."

"Mr. McCord is right, and please let everyone you come across know we will still have our Independence Day celebration in the meadow this evening."

Nettie bobbed her head, made her excuses, and said goodbye. Evelyn watched her leave and noticed Nettie now walked with a lighter step. To Cooper she said, "I've always found telling one or two women any news in town ensures it will reach everyone. Nettie has already proven to have a fondness for socializing."

Cooper's mouth lifted up at the edges. "You mean gossip."

"Socializing sounds better."

"Uh-huh. What's wrong? You looked fierce walking toward us before."

"You saw me?"

Cooper nodded. "Briefly before Mrs. Sandstrom demanded my full attention."

Evelyn walked toward the schoolhouse. "You must be on your way to see Abigail. I was looking for Daniel and then I saw you coming here. I hoped you knew where he had gone."

"To the mine. He rode out a few minutes ago, but I can bring him back." Cooper relayed to her what he and Daniel had discussed and their conclusion that

Jacob's death was likely the result of a snake bite and unfortunate fall. He explained Daniel's mission to the mine to see if anyone had decided to not show up for work, perhaps having left with a new horse.

"That is a tremendous relief. I am sorry for young Jacob, but the thought of someone we know—"

"Those were our sentiments, too. Now, what brought you out here looking for Daniel?"

"Gordon is missing."

Cooper stopped, forcing Evelyn to stop, too, or walk into him. "When?"

"I don't know exactly. I was in the kitchen, he must have left by the back door. I took a tray of food upstairs so they could eat and continue resting. Hany and Grace were still asleep and neither heard him leave." Evelyn moved her eyes over the school's white-washed front door when it opened. Abigail stepped outside and waved. "I would go for Daniel myself—"

"I'll be able to catch him before he reaches the mine. Please explain to Abigail for me and tell her . . . tell her I won't be long."

Cooper moved quickly on his feet, reaching his horse by the time Abigail stepped alongside Evelyn and looped her arm through hers.

"Where is he off to in such a rush?"

"To fetch Daniel."

Evelyn subjected herself to Abigail's scrutiny when her sister forced her to turn. "Is everything all right?"

"I'm not sure." Evelyn patted her sister's hand so she would ease her grasp. "It will be, I know that much. Cooper won't be long. I would not have asked him to go if it wasn't important. He has been anxious to see you since this morning."

Abigail's rose-tinged cheeks darkened with her blush. "I have been eager to see him, too. I am used to his hunting excursions, but it is becoming more difficult to be apart from . . ." Abigail's blush lightened when her words faltered. "I'm so sorry, Evie. You know more than anyone what it is like, and here I am complaining of a few days."

"There is no need to worry or apologize, Abigail. I've had Daniel back home and in my arms for almost three months now. Soon those four years will be a faded memory." Evelyn doubted the truth of her words the second she thought them, though they brought comfort to say them aloud.

"Will you tell me what's wrong, Evie?"

Distracted by the comings and goings of people, Evelyn murmured an affirmative to her sister. Her focus, however, remained on the front of her house. From where she stood in the meadow with Abigail, she could see part of gardens, the porch, and the rise of the barn behind the house. If she moved a few feet to the left, the mercantile would block her view. As it happened, she glimpsed enough to make her curious. "I must go. I promise to explain everything soon, but I need to check on someone."

"Evie." Abigail held fast to her arm. "Did someone kill Jacob or was it an accident? Harriet believes someone murdered him and heard as much from someone—she failed to mention who—before she arrived at the school."

"Harriett's information has gaps." Evelyn shouldn't have been surprised, and yet sometimes the network of news through town marveled even her. She did not want to speculate on who took the trouble to rush to tell Harriett of the goings-on. Evelyn recalled the reassuring words Cooper gave her. "After further investigation, it's believed it was a tragic accident. There is no reason for anyone to worry anymore. I promise, all will be well. School is letting out early today, yes?"

Abigail nodded. "The children are making decorations and practicing lines for the songs they plan to sing tonight. Harriett said the celebration will continue."

"How she heard already is baffling. Yes, our plans have not changed. Well, not entirely. Don't be late tonight."

With those parting words, Evelyn left her sister to hurry home. Haste was not easily achieved when people stopped her progression. She rushed through assurances the best she could but quickly disengaged herself from each conversation. When she arrived at the house, she stopped on the porch, her hand ready to open the front door. The sobbing on the other side of the door, or more precisely, through one of the open windows in her sitting room, gave Evelyn pause. It was the unexpected voice that prompted her expedited entry into the house.

She found Gordon holding his wife and daughter in his wide embrace. They were slight enough for his arms to encircle them both and hold them close. Gordon's eyes met hers when she stepped into the room.

"I's sorry, Mrs. Whitcomb. Hany done told me I scared de life out of her."

Evelyn's pounding heart slowed with each step closer to the family. She stopped five feet away, not wanting to encroach. She would have preferred to leave them alone entirely, only it was imperative she speak with Gordon.

"Daniel should be here soon." Evelyn cast a furtive glance to Grace before asking, "Where did you go, Gordon, and why did you not say anything?"

"I can explain."

Evelyn realized her mistake. "I am not upset, but like your family, I worried for your safety. Cooper told me that he and Daniel believe they can prove the young man this morning died by an accident, but until they can find the men who accused you, and explain what happened, you are safer here."

Gordon leaned his head low to his wife's ear and whispered, meant only for her. Hany nodded, gathered Grace in her arms, and urged the young girl from the room. When they had left, Gordon faced Evelyn with all the contrition of a man on his way to the gallows.

"You got a right to be angry, Mrs. Whitcomb. Hany sure is."

Evelyn felt her mouth twitch. "Hany was worried, too."

"I should've told you. Hany lost her locket. I saw it missing and it was her mama's. Didn't seem right to leave it out in dem woods."

A deep breath filled Evelyn's lungs, and when she released it, the tension in her body went with it. "That was thoughtful of you, Gordon. I'm sure Hany appreciated your effort in retrieving such a precious item. Did you find it?"

Gordon nodded. "I figured where she might of lost it. She stumbled gettin' out of de wagon. I figure I'd be back inside 'afore anyone noticed."

They both looked to the open, front door when they heard the pounding of hooves on the hard-packed dirt road. Only one rider, Evelyn surmised, and as though she had memorized the sound of Daniel's unique step, she knew it was him before she glanced out the window.

DANIEL HALTED ONCE INSIDE and examined the scene before him. Gordon appeared guilty and Evelyn's face expressed relief. Cooper had known only what Evelyn told him, that Gordon was missing.

"I feared the worst, friend." Daniel held out his hand and waited for Gordon to accept it. They stepped back again. "It is your business if you come and go, and not ours, but with your wife and child left behind, you must have known everyone would worry about you."

Evelyn linked her arm with his, drawing some of his frustration away. "It is all right, Daniel. Gordon explained that he left only to search for Hany's locket. She lost it somewhere when exiting the wagon. The mistake was mine, in fearing he had gone, when he was just near the barn. If I had not alerted Hany and Grace that he was not here, they likely would have remained asleep."

"I should've said somethin', Mrs. Whitcomb."

Daniel listened to his wife's self-recrimination and Daniel's apology. He understood why Gordon went on his errand without telling anyone, just as he understood Evelyn's concern when Gordon was not where she thought he should be.

Daniel whispered to his wife, "I need to speak with Gordon, for only a few minutes." He looked at his friend. "Would you walk with me outside? We won't be long."

Gordon nodded and followed Daniel out the front door. Daniel waited until Gordon fell into step beside him when his instinct would have been to walk behind. They walked the trail leading toward the creek before Daniel spoke. "A week after I came home, Evelyn came to our room expecting to find me. She insisted I rest and was bringing me a tray of food. What she found was an empty bed and room. I had left the house without telling her, much like you did. I was not accustomed to explaining myself to anyone except my commanding officer. Unfortunately, I saw the effect of my blunder when I returned two hours later from a walk. Since then, I make sure to tell her where I am or where I will be going."

He stopped by the creek and for a few seconds remained silent so only the sound of the water smoothing over rocks filled the air. "Evelyn's reaction was more likely an echo of what she felt that day, and nothing you did wrong. I explain this only because I know why you said nothing to her when you went outside. You were born into slavery, and not a moment of your life has gone by when you didn't have to account for it. You've earned your freedom, Gordon. Do not feel guilty for using it. Please, we only hope you will be careful until the matter with Jacob Smith is resolved. It won't take much longer for everyone to hear that you are not to blame."

Gordon stared, not saying a single word for two minutes. "Hany says I still gots to say sorry again to Mrs. Whitcomb. If Hany wants somethin'—"

"Hany will get it." Daniel's chuckle mingled with the sound of lapping water. "Come, friend. Let us return. I still have a task to see to."

"I wants to help, if I can."

"Stay at the house and keep the women happy knowing they won't have any more worries today. You would be helping a lot."

Gordon grinned. "Ain't dat de truth."

DANIEL KISSED HIS WIFE. Hard and fast. He swung onto the back of his horse and returned to the mine to complete his earlier errand. The morning had moved into afternoon, and under the brighter sun, people set up makeshift tables in the meadow. Word had spread that the celebration would continue, which meant Cooper had told someone that Jacob's death was an accident. All it took was telling one person.

Accidents happened daily in the wilderness. They did all right without a town doctor, but people still died from injuries and illness. What happened to Jacob was unfortunate and made worse that he died on their day of independence. One could look upon it as Jacob's liberation from this life into a better one. Daniel had lost friends in battle and found some comfort believing they passed on to a more desirable place, free of pestilence, hunger, and eventual death. He was grateful Fate had spared him, and he owed his existence to sheer luck and Evelyn.

He arrived at the mine and slowed his horse to a meander and finally stopped him at a rise before the road eased down. The placer gold mine had not been boom-to-bust as expected. The gold was separated from the topsoil by running it through sluices, leaving the heavier gold pieces to sink while the dirt and lighter particles washed away with the water. They had been successful for a year before deciding they needed to find an alternative method for when the gold was no longer easy to find.

When Cooper first showed Daniel the mine and explained how they began digging and hauling, Daniel marveled at what had been accomplished during his time away. His inheritance had bought the land and built the town, but it was the hard work and ingenuity of the people that allowed it to prosper.

He had only one condition on continuing the mine—that the landscape would not be destroyed. If the time came when tunneling became too dangerous, they would close the mine rather than resort to hydraulic mining. Daniel had seen the effects of it on the environment and refused to destroy their land in such a manner.

Studying the operation below him, Daniel silently thanked Evelyn and Cooper for agreeing with him. When the mine eventually closed down, as was the natural order of mines, they would work to restore to the land close to its former beauty.

The foreman, Jedediah Cosgrove, waved Daniel down when he spotted him on the rise. They had made Jedediah foreman two months prior when the previous foreman decided he had suffered enough from Montana winters. He was bound for Arizona one week later and they offered Jedediah the job. He still limped from a bullet to the thigh the doctors decided not to remove, but he had proven himself to be a fair supervisor and administrator, respected by the other men.

Daniel dismounted and shook Jedediah's hand. "We don't see you here often, Mr. Whitcomb. You here about Jacob?"

Daniel nodded, keeping his focus on the men working. "Did Abraham tell you?"

"No, it wasn't him. Abe didn't show up today. Neville told me. Said he saw Abe bring the slave into town who killed the boy."

"There are no more slaves in this country, Jedediah, and there aren't any in Whitcomb Springs."

Jedediah removed his hat and wiped his sweaty brow with a dusty rag. "Sorry about that. Still getting used to the idea."

Daniel ignored the man's bigotry for the moment. "A snake bit Jacob. Cooper found the evidence on Jacob's arm. The conclusion is that Jacob fell from his horse, too sick to ride, and hit his head. Either way, he was unlikely to survive the bite."

"I was sorry to hear about Jacob. He was a good boy and hard worker. I'll make sure to end the speculating."

"Good." Daniel pulled himself easily into the saddle again and looked down at his foreman. "And release the men from work for the rest of the day. Tonight's celebration will still happen and they need help in town to set up. Anyone here now will receive a full day's wage."

"The men will appreciate it, sir."

"And Jedediah. Did Neville happen to say if he knew where Abe was going?"

Jedediah lifted his shoulders in a shrug, his face showing equal confusion. "He wasn't scheduled to work a shift today. I reckoned he was at home or in town."

Daniel thanked the man and rode back to town. Abe lived in one of the row houses built for the miners soon after Cooper discovered gold in their creek. One row of compact houses was nestled in a small clearing halfway between town and the mine. Most of the married men built small houses and cabins in town, or closer, for the safety and convenience of their wives and children. Daniel stopped there on his return trip to find Abe's place empty. He had not believed Abe would be at home, nor did he expect to find him anywhere else.

He rode the few miles home and noticed the scent of a fire already burning. The townspeople had accomplished a lot in the hour he'd been gone, and those already at the meadow would soon be joined by the men from the mine and timber camp. Each man worked only five days a week and never more hours than was healthy. Daniel decided to ask Cooper to have the foremen close down both sites tomorrow so the men could enjoy the remainder of the day without worrying about rising early. In their town, they couldn't get into much trouble. Maggie cut off drinks after three at the saloon, so if anyone planned to get drunk, it wouldn't be in town.

Meat would begin to roast over the flames and in another hour, the official festivities would begin. It had been Daniel's idea not to cancel, but now that the time of celebration neared, his apprehension rose to the surface. He backtracked and returned to the clinic, nodded to the two men still standing watch to make sure the body wasn't disturbed, and entered the building.

He crossed the wood floor and gently eased the canvas down and away from Jacob's head. "It was dumb luck that took you, but you deserved better. It was a hell of a way to go, Jacob. You made through the worst of the battles only to be felled by a damn snake. There are enough of us here, enough of us who made it out, to give you a proper send-off tomorrow." Daniel covered Jacob again, left the building, and rode home.

EVELYN SMOOTHED THE BODICE of her dress. She

had become used to foregoing a tight corset since leaving Pennsylvania, but tonight the dress would not close properly without tightened laces. Hany, thankfully, had been willing to assist. When she finished helping Evelyn into her dress, Hany left the room with a smile that left Evelyn wondering.

She turned to the right and left, examining her reflection from every angle. Her stomach and hips were still trim thanks to all the hard work in the gardens. She had grown stronger, but the change in her body was subtle. Evelyn smoothed her hands again over the delicate muslin and watched her eyes widen. Her waist had not thickened, but it did not take a lot for her body to fight against the seams of a carefully fitted gown. Her shock shifted to pleasure when she realized the meaning behind Hany's grin.

She and Daniel had spoken of starting a family, but that was before the war. When Evelyn didn't become pregnant, they wondered if it would ever happen for them. She knew with all her heart that Daniel would be as wonderful of a father as he had been a husband. "Is he ready?" She whispered the words aloud as she held her hands to her belly. "Am I ready?" Their time together since his return had been filled with days and nights relearning what they'd once known, and discovering new traits, likes, and dislikes they'd developed during their time apart. They were still the same people who imagined a house filled with children, but were they truly ready?

Evelyn fortified herself with a few deep breaths. Excitement and apprehension warred for first place in her thoughts, and it was a few more minutes before she guarded her emotions enough to descend the steps. Daniel waited at the bottom of the staircase, and nearby stood Gordon, Hany, and Grace. Evelyn had procured clothing for them from the general store that reasonably fit without alterations. It was Daniel's attire that caused her to falter and grip the bannister.

Daniel held out his hand and helped her down the final four steps. For her hearing only, he said, "You look magnificent."

"So do you." Since his return, Daniel's fine suits never left the armoire. The man before her looked more like the man she married. His eyes stood out as different. They'd seen much and revealed his suffering even when he tried to hide it. Tonight, his pain appeared to leave him alone, for in his eyes Evelyn saw only love.

"I cannot help but feel guilty with Jacob lying at the clinic while the rest of us celebrate."

"Do not worry about Jacob, my love. This is for him, too." Daniel did not elaborate and instead turned her attention to the others. "Gordon worries about his presence at the celebration tonight. I have assured him it is his choice, though perhaps some encouragement from you will help."

Evelyn walked two steps toward Gordon and his small family. "I have been false to all three of you, and to my husband. I have made assumptions about what your lives were like, about what you've endured. I told myself that I need only feel sympathy to understand, and yet the truth is, I know nothing. I cannot understand and I will not insult you by trying to imagine it. Whether it was chance or Fate that brought you here on this day, I will not speculate. This is a day for freedom and a time for healing. I know the establishment of our nation so long ago may not mean the same for you as it does for us—yet. However, I hope you will come to think of it as a day of hopeful beginnings."

Hany fingered the buttons on her new dress and looked shyly at Evelyn. "I don't reckon all folks will think like you."

"No, I suspect they won't, except here. In this town, every honorable person is welcome and has the chance to begin anew. You, my dear friends, are honorable people."

Hany tried to hide her sniffle. Young Grace did not

fully grasp the meaning of what everyone said, but by the sweet smile and gentle tug on her mother's hand, Evelyn guessed that Grace understood happiness well enough.

THEY ARRIVED IN THE meadow walking side by side with the Wells family. Silence descended on the crowd as all eyes, young and old, settled on their group. A few murmurs made the rounds until they were silenced by clapping. When Daniel looked from person to person, he realized they all watched the Wells family, and it was them they were honoring.

Not everyone joined in, and some dissention was to be expected, but Gordon, Hany, and Grace had been accepted. Daniel knew it was because they came as his and Evelyn's guests. He only cared that it was a start.

The townspeople had come together to enjoy good food, company, and a commemoration of independence. Tonight, there were no enemies, no sides, only friends and countrymen. The children sang "The Star-Spangled Banner" and "Amazing Grace," assisted by several adults. The first song roused the crowd, while the second cast a calm over everyone.

It was after the final lyrics to "Amazing Grace" ended that Daniel called on everyone to raise their glasses—with whatever filled them—to Jacob Smith, once a soldier and always a brother.

Toward the end of the evening, Daniel noticed his wife's distraction. "You're looking for someone?"

"Abigail. When Gordon returned, I went back to the school to speak with her. She wasn't there. I haven't seen her all afternoon."

"I suspect she's with Cooper. He had something he wanted to ask her."

Evelyn's arm was already linked with his and now her hand grasped his forearm. "Abigail has said nothing to me."

"I do not believe she knows."

"I had not realized. I mean, I knew it would happen. They love each other, and I already consider Cooper family, but it hasn't been long enough. They've only known—"

Daniel silenced her with a gentle kiss. "When there is never an assurance of tomorrow, it has been long enough."

"Cooper said nothing to me, either. Did he speak with you? There would not have been time to ask our father, and—"

Daniel figured what worked once would work again so he kissed her into silence. When their lips parted this time, Evelyn remained quiet, eliciting his grin.

Daniel thought of his conversation with Cooper on the mountain only that morning. He had declared his love for Abigail, and for Daniel, that was enough. "Yes," he said. "You will be happy for them, won't you?"

"Of course!" Evelyn wrapped her arms around Daniel's neck, not caring who might see. "You're right, there is no need for them to wait a moment longer. She is my younger sister, though, so allow me a little anxiety on her behalf."

Daniel chuckled and noticed the objects of their conversation walking toward them. Abigail wore a beaming smile that brightened every inch of her face. Cooper was in much the same predicament. "Evie, love, turn around." She did, and the sisters embraced. Both allowed their tears of happiness to fall unbidden, and Evelyn was relentless until Abigail promised they would talk more in a few days.

Tomorrow they would hold Jacob's funeral.

Cooper pulled Daniel aside when Evelyn and Abigail were occupied congratulating the children on their beautiful songs. Cooper explained what he found in the search for Jacob's horse. "A farmer who lives a quarter mile west of town, Zeb Calhoun, saw a rider headed out pretty fast. He couldn't see much where he stood in his field, but he thinks the horse was a buckskin, like Jacob's. I followed the tracks but that road is well traveled."

"Without a telegraph, we have no way to get word quickly to the nearest towns. A letter with a description, mailed to the neighboring areas, will have to suffice."

Cooper nodded. "Any word on when Abbott Jenkins will arrive?"

"Any day now. Although, you've made a pretty good stand-in sheriff." Daniel chuckled at Cooper's genuine groan.

"I'm not cut out to be accountable to people on a daily basis."

"What about Abigail?"

Cooper blinked. "Well, shoot."

Daniel and Cooper both shifted their gazes to Abigail when Daniel asked, "Having second thoughts?"

The smile on Cooper's face told Daniel everything he ever needed to believe his friend and sister-in-law were as true and real as he and Evelyn. Cooper walked away from Daniel, stopping only long enough to say, "It will please me to be accountable to Abigail every day for the rest of our lives together." He quickly qualified it with, "But only Abigail."

LATER THAT EVENING, WHEN they all returned to the

big house Daniel had built for Evelyn, they lay together in bed, limbs entwined. Daniel brought Evelyn even closer to his chest and inhaled the sweet fragrance clinging to her soft hair. "I have been thinking about the house across the road from us."

"The one James Bair built?"

Daniel nodded, thinking of his friend and one of the founders of Whitcomb Springs. He perished his first winter in Montana, and his house had remained empty since. "Do you think it would be a good place for a family?"

"Yes, I do. The Wells family could be very happy there. It's been kept in good repair and only requires a thorough cleaning. James only had a few pieces of furniture. We can bring in more."

"We could, though I think Gordon will want to build most of it himself."

"He's a craftsman?"

Daniel kissed the back of her head. Closer wasn't close enough for him. "He told me he built a few pieces for the family who owned him."

"Whitcomb Springs could use a man with his talents."

"Uh-huh." Daniel's hands moved from her hips, inching higher. "Evie. When were you going to tell me?"

He felt her stiffen for a second, then relax before she rolled onto her other side and faced him. "When I was certain. I only realized it today." She covered his hand when it moved to her flat belly. "How did you know?"

Daniel leaned in and brushed his lips over hers. Once. Twice. "I know your body better than you do. Some parts have . . ."

"Don't you say it, Daniel Whitcomb."

"In the presence of a lady, I wouldn't dare."

She laughed and swatted his shoulder. "Yes, you would dare."

Daniel sobered. He caressed Evelyn's cheek, her arm, and moved his fingers up and down the length of her, wherever he could reach. "I don't want you to have any regrets." He pressed a finger to mouth, preventing her from speaking. "Let me say this. I still have nightmares. Not as often, but they come when I least expect. The night I nearly choked you in my sleep was the worst night of my life."

"No." Evelyn rolled up and straddled him, forcing his arms back. It was her way of gaining his full attention, and she had it. "That was not you. You woke up before any harm was done."

"I don't want to be a danger to you or our child."

"Do you really believe you will be?"

Daniel leaned up, pressing against Evelyn's grip on

his arms until she released them. His hands found a comfortable place on the small of her back. "No. I am getting better. You've been more patient than I had a right to ask. I know there is still more for me to deal with, and one day—soon I hope—I will tell you what I haven't been able to share yet. One thing I know with absolute certainty is that I will never harm you again or our child, even during my worst nightmares. But it's important you know I will never—"

Evelyn's lips found his and swept him up in a kiss that evaporated all reason from his mind. Against his mouth, she murmured, "I never thought it. I had a moment today, wondering if we were ready, but I never once doubted your ability to be a father. You are the most honorable and loving man I have ever known. Our children will be blessed to have you."

Daniel shook his head and flipped his wife onto her back. "To have us."

THE FOLLOWING MORNING, DANIEL donned his officer's uniform. Evelyn stared in awe at how marvelous he looked. She had cleaned and pressed the garments and found a place for them in the armoire, but he had not worn it for her before today.

She did not have to wonder why Daniel's

countenance shined brighter today than other since his return. He had overcome the first of his internal demons, and the chains of fear and grim memories would continue to unravel, one day at a time. It would be a day of sadness and celebration as they lay Jacob Smith to rest in the town cemetery. And yet, Jacob would be remembered more for his passing because of the timing of his unplanned departure. Evelyn did not know how so much love could take place on a day of mourning, yet love filled her.

She and Abigail had a wedding to plan, and God willing, the child she carried would come safely into the world. Every dream and plan they had envisioned when they first stood atop the mountain and saw their untouched valley had been for this moment.

"Evelyn?"

She smiled at herself in the mirror as though she and her reflection shared a secret. "Coming, darling." Evelyn draped a paisley, silk shawl over her black dress and went to meet her husband so they could honor not only one soldier, but all who fell and all who returned.

The End . . . and another hopeful beginning.

Want more? Journey to the little mountain town of Whitcomb Springs, Montana, and meet a delightful group of settlers whose stories and adventures celebrate the rich life of the American West. Read stories from MK McClintock, Samantha St. Claire, Christi Corbett, and Lynn Winchester.

Thank you for reading "Unchained Courage"! I hope you enjoyed the story; there's more to come.

Don't miss out on future books and stories in the Whitcomb Springs series:
www.mkmcclintock.com/subscribe.

Interested in reading more by MK McClintock?

The Historical Western Romance
Montana Gallagher series:
Gallagher's Pride
Gallagher's Hope
Gallagher's Choice
An Angel Called Gallagher
Journey to Hawk's Peak

Historical Western & Western Romance
Crooked Creek series:
"Emma of Crooked Creek"
"Hattie of Crooked Creek"
"Briley of Crooked Creek"
"Clara of Crooked Creek"

Historical Romantic Mystery
British Agent series:
Alaina Claiborne
Blackwood Crossing
Clayton's Honor

Enjoy her collection of heartwarming Christmas short stories any time of the year: *A Home for Christmas*

THE AUTHOR

AWARD-WINNING AUTHOR MK McClintock is devoted to giving her readers books laced with adventure, romance, and a touch of mystery. Her novels and short stories take you from the rugged mountains of Montana to the Victorian British Isles, all with good helpings of daring exploits and endearing love stories. She enjoys a peaceful life in the Rocky Mountains where she is writing her next book.

Learn more about MK by visiting her website and blog: www.mkmcclintock.com.

Made in the USA
Las Vegas, NV
07 November 2022

58988799R00042